KIDS CAN'T STOP READING THE *CHOOSE YOUR OWN ADVENTURE*™ STORIES!

"I like *Choose Your Own Adventure*™ books because they're full of surprises. I can't wait to read more."
—Cary Romanos, age 12

"Makes you think thoroughly before making a decision."
—Hassan Stevenson, age 11

"I read five different stories in one night and that's a record for me. The different endings are fun."
—Timmy Sullivan, age 9

"It's great fun! I like the idea of making my own decisions."
—Anthony Ziccardi, age 11

AND TEACHERS LIKE THIS SERIES, TOO!

"We have read and reread, worn thin, loved, loaned, bought for others, and donated to school libraries, the *Choose Your Own Adventure*™ books."

CHOOSE YOUR OWN ADVENTURE™— AND MAKE READING MORE FUN!

Bantam Books in the Choose Your Own Adventure™ Series
Ask your bookseller for the books you have missed

#1 THE CAVE OF TIME by Edward Packard

#2 JOURNEY UNDER THE SEA by R.A. Montgomery

#3 BY BALLOON TO THE SAHARA by D. Terman

#4 SPACE AND BEYOND by R.A. Montgomery

#5 THE MYSTERY OF CHIMNEY ROCK
by Edward Packard

#6 YOUR CODE NAME IS JONAH by Edward Packard

#7 THE THIRD PLANET FROM ALTAIR
by Edward Packard

#8 DEADWOOD CITY by Edward Packard

#9 WHO KILLED HARLOWE THROMBEY?
by Edward Packard

#10 THE LOST JEWELS OF NABOOTI
by R.A. Montgomery

#11 MYSTERY OF THE MAYA by R.A. Montgomery

CHOOSE YOUR OWN ADVENTURE™ · 11

MYSTERY OF THE MAYA

BY R. A. MONTGOMERY

ILLUSTRATED BY RICHARD ANDERSON

BANTAM BOOKS
TORONTO · NEW YORK · LONDON · SYDNEY

RL 5, IL 5+

MYSTERY OF THE MAYA

A Bantam Book / May 1981

Choose Your Own Adventure is *a trademark of Bantam Books, Inc.*

Cover art by Paul Granger.

ISBN 0-553-14600-9

Published simultaneously in the United States and Canada

Bantam Books are published by Bantam Books, Inc. Its trademark, consisting of the words "Bantam Books" and the portrayal of a Bantam, is Registered in U.S. Patent and Trademark Office and in other countries. Marca Registrada. Bantam Books, Inc., 666 Fifth Avenue, New York, New York 10103.

PRINTED IN THE UNITED STATES OF AMERICA

0 9 8 7 6 5 4

This book is dedicated to
Anson & Ramsey

and

A special thanks to Judy Gitenstein, my editor,
for her continued energy and support.

WARNING!!!!

Do not read this book straight through from beginning to end! These pages contain many different adventures you can have in the Mexican jungle. Some of the adventures take place in the present time, some in the past, and others in the future. From time to time as you read along, you will be asked to make decisions and choices. Some of them are dangerous!

The adventures you take are a result of your choice. *You* are responsible because *you* choose. After you make your choice, follow the instructions to see what happens to you next.

Think carefully before you make a move. One mistake can be your last . . . or it *may* lead you to fame and fortune!

Turn to page 1.

You are a writer on assignment to travel to Mexico to explore the ruins of the Mayan Indians. Your editor in New York hopes you will gather enough information to write a book about why the Mayan civilization collapsed.

It's a tough assignment. No one really knows what happened to the Mayan people. Several thousand years ago, the Mayas were a powerful people. They lived in the jungle and along the coast of the eastern part of Mexico, now called the Yucatan. They were excellent mathematicians, astronomers and engineers. Like the Egyptians, they built enormous pyramids. They surrounded the pyramids with other stone buildings and temples and observatories. No one knows how they were able to drag the huge

Go on to page 2.

blocks of stone many miles to the building sites. The Mayas were successful farmers, too. They were able to turn jungle into farmland. It seemed they could do anything.

Then, suddenly, as if an electric plug had been pulled, the Mayan civilization collapsed. The people fled from the cities into the surrounding land. Farms were overgrown. The jungle took over. The glory of the Mayan people had vanished overnight.

What happened? Some say a plague killed many people; some say there was a horrible war; others believe the crops failed and the Mayan people starved. Were their gods angry? Was there a sudden lack of water; or, was it something really strange, like visitors from another planet taking their leaders away? No one knows—for sure. The failure of the Mayan civilization has been a mystery for 800 years. It's now your job to find out what happened.

Your plane has just landed at the airport outside Merida, capital of the Yucatan and the largest city near the ruins. Stepping down from the plane, you gaze out on low, flat land with scrubby, dull green jungle. The yellow sun is hot, and the air is clear. You take out a small brown notebook and jot down your first impressions of this strange land. Your felt-tipped pen squeaks across the page as you describe tangled jungle, the sticky heat, the brilliant sun.

The job ahead of you is a big and difficult one. Historians and archeologists have tried to solve the mystery, but no one has really succeeded.

You were told by your editor that a guide named Manuel would meet you at the airport. A short, dark-skinned man dressed in white pants and a brightly patterned red, yellow, and blue shirt greets you.

"Hello, my name is Manuel. I am to be your guide. Welcome to Mexico."

Go on to page 4.

His skin is like copper. His large nose and sloping forehead remind you of paintings and stone carvings you have seen of the Mayas. Suddenly you realize that he is one of the descendants of the ancient Mayan tribes. The civilization may have collapsed 800 years ago but the people live on to this day.

You like Manuel immediately and you feel that he is going to be a great help in your search.

"May I suggest that we visit Dr. Lopez at the university? He is an authority on the Mayan civilization. Or perhaps you would prefer to just go ahead and visit the ruins."

If you want to visit Dr. Lopez, turn to page 5.

If you want to go to the ruins, turn to page 11.

Manuel smiles with satisfaction at your choice. "Fine. You will like Dr. Lopez. Come with me."

A taxi takes you through the narrow streets of Merida, past Spanish-style buildings and onto a broad avenue lined by palm trees. The taxi pulls up in front of a yellow stone building. It is the university, and Dr. Lopez has an office on the fourth floor. You enter the room and he speaks.

"Welcome. Welcome to Merida, and welcome to the Mayas." Dr. Lopez is an old man, stoop-shouldered, with white hair, heavy black-rimmed glasses, and skin that reminds you of shoe leather. His office is filled with pottery and carvings of snakes and fierce-looking half-human, half-animal forms.

Go on to page 6.

"What are you looking for?" Dr. Lopez asks you.

"I want to find out about the Mayas. Why they failed. What happened to them. Can you help me?"

Dr. Lopez looks at Manuel and smiles a secret and mysterious smile.

"Well, my friend. You have come to the right place at the right time. Here we have a secret time potion developed by the Mayas hundreds of years ago." He holds up a small bottle. "We believe they used it to travel in time and in space. Don't be afraid. I've used it, and I'm still here."

You stare at the old man in disbelief, but his warm smile and kindly face encourage you.

"Drink the potion and go back in time 800 years to see the glory of the Mayas." He hands you the small green bottle. You shake with fear, but what an opportunity.

"Don't worry. Manuel will go with you."

If you decide to drink the potion and travel back in time, turn to page 7.

If you decline the potion and decide to visit the ruins without benefit of the trip into the past, turn to page 11.

The potion is thick and dark green, almost like the slime you find in stagnant pools in the jungle. The smell, though, is light and sweet and fragrant. You take a gulp and put the bottle with the rest of the potion into your pocket, next to your notebook.

Suddenly, you are surrounded by people dressed in the bright red and green and gold clothes of the ancient Mayas. You are no longer in Dr. Lopez's study in Merida. You are in Uxmal, standing in front of the huge pyramid called the Temple of the Magicians. It seems to command all the other buildings as it rises steeply out of the jungle.

Manuel is beside you. His red, yellow, and blue shirt blend in with the brilliant Mayan colors. "Don't be frightened," he whispers. "We are 1500 years back in time."

Across from the Temple of the Magicians is a long, low building made of a yellowish-white stone covered with the same snake and man-animal carvings you saw in Dr. Lopez's study. The building looks as if it contains long hallways and many small, dark rooms.

Suddenly, a hush falls over the crowd of Mayas. Five men and a woman in gold and red robes, carrying silver spears and wearing bright green feathers in their hair move through the crowd and start climbing slowly up the steps of the Temple of the Magicians. They must be priests and a priestess because the people bow down in front of them. In the courtyard below is a squad of soldiers carrying knives and bows and arrows. They look angry.

8

Go on to page 10.

Manuel must be one of the ruling clan, for people bow down before him also. He smiles and says, "My friend, you may choose to go with the priests and priestess or you can go with the warriors. Both groups will teach you a great deal about the Mayan civilization."

You are so busy taking notes about everything around you that you hardly hear what he says. Manuel repeats the question.

If you follow the priests and priestess,
turn to page 12.

If you follow the warriors, turn to page 13.

You and Manuel drive to your hotel in Merida. Once you arrive, you stand at your window, looking out over the rooftops and palm trees to the scrubby jungle and plains that surround the town. Broad avenues lined with large trees, spacious squares with carved fountains, and large haciendas behind high walls characterize the city. Merida was founded by the Spanish after the conquest in the sixteenth century, and old churches and fortresses add to the Spanish flavor.

Manuel comes to your room and invites you to dinner.

"Tomorrow we begin," he says. "We can travel to the ruins. They are very beautiful."

You ask him which one you should visit first.

He tells you that Chichen Itza is the youngest and largest site of Mayan ruins. The central points of interest are a huge pyramid, which dominates the area; a domed observatory, sitting silently near the jungle; and the deep water hole or *cenote.* There, too, is the famed and feared ball court. In ancient times, the losers of the ball game also lost their lives.

Uxmal, while smaller than Chichen Itza, is far older. The stone used for building there has been cut and carved in delicate patterns. The Temple of the Magicians at Uxmal is smaller than the temple at Chichen Itza but is impressive as it rises out of the jungle.

"It's up to you," Manuel says.

If you go to Chichen Itza, turn to page 16.

If you go to Uxmal, turn to page 15.

The priestess watches you closely as the five priests form a tight square. Their long, black hair is covered with a sticky evil-smelling substance. You ask Manuel what it is.

"Blood. It is the blood of victims of the sacrifices. The priests think it makes them stronger. You will see."

You pull back in horror.

"Sacrifices? What for? What kind of sacrifices?"

Manuel says, "Be patient. Just follow the priests. They know you are going with them. Don't be frightened."

That may be easy for him to say, but you are scared. The head priest signals you to follow. They lead you up the steep steps of the Temple of the Magicians. At the top is a small room. Inside the room is a stone altar stained with brownish, dried blood. There is still some blood in a bowl on the altar.

"You are now going to be one of us," says the head priest. You're not sure that's what you want to do.

If you want to escape, turn to page 18.

If you decide to stay and accept their offer of priesthood, turn to page 21.

The warriors in the courtyard are practicing with bow and arrow, spear and club. They are a noisy group, bragging and shouting, punching, and wrestling.

Manuel tells you these warriors have come from Chichen Itza. He introduces you to the officer in charge. On your way back to Chichen Itza, the officer speaks to you.

"There are two groups here. One group raids our enemies to get slaves or take revenge. They are fast, quiet in the jungle, and ready to die if captured. The other group defends us against invaders. They are careful and watchful. They never give up. They will fight until the last one is dead."

Go on to page 14.

"Who are your enemies?" you ask.

"Toltecs, a savage group who worship Smoking Mirror, their god of war and death. They are always invading us." Several warriors with you nod in agreement. You still have your notebook and you write down notes about the Toltecs. You are careful not to let them see the pen or notebook. You could never explain what they are.

You find out that there are fights between the Mayas caused by jealousies and long resentments.

The officer in command says, "It's up to you, you can go on the raids or stay here in defense."

If you join the raiding party, turn to page 22.

If you choose to stay, turn to page 23.

You walk with Manuel to the bus station for the trip to Uxmal. The pavement shimmers with heat, and the smells of garlic and spicy food hang in the air.

The bus trip is long and hot, but finally you arrive at the ruins of Uxmal. The Temple of the Magicians looms over the land. Steep stone steps ascend to a smaller temple building on top of the pyramid. Across from the Temple of the Magicians is a large, rectangular building which the Spanish Conquistadors called the Nunnery, but no one really knows what it was used for.

"What do you think, Manuel? I mean, what was it used for? Any ideas?"

Manuel hesitates for a minute and says, "Perhaps the building was the palace of the priests. Perhaps they lived there. Perhaps they conducted experiments there. I don't know."

Crowds of people are milling around the ruins. You wish that you could be alone. Where should you start, at the Temple of the Magicians or the Nunnery?

If you investigate the Temple of the Magicians, turn to page 25.

If you investigate the Nunnery, turn to page 26.

The highway to Chichen Itza runs through flat, scrubby land. A few houses or huts line the road. Then you see it from the bus. It almost jumps out of the low-lying jungle—EL CASTILLO—the giant pyramid looms above you.

Around El Castillo are broad avenues leading to other stone buildings, to courtyards, and to the evil ball court where Mayas lost their lives if they lost the game. One avenue leads to the *cenote* or giant well. This deep *cenote* that sinks thirty feet from ground level to the surface of its water has taken the lives of many sacrificial victims.

A few tourists mill around. A group of about twenty people stand quietly at the base of El Castillo. You ask Manuel what they are doing, what they are waiting for. He gives a knowing smile and says, "Soon you will see for yourself. Look up at the top of the pyramid."

Your eyes follow his pointing finger. The top of the pyramid is glowing with a bright red color! Where is it coming from?

"Watch, my friend. This is worth waiting for."

Then you see it. A large spacecraft hovers over the pyramid, shoots out a transporter beam, and waits.

"What does it mean, Manuel? What's happening?" You are frightened.

"These Mayan ruins are contact points for other planets. That group of people has been chosen to leave Earth for the planet, Merganatic."

You believe in UFOs, but now that you are seeing one, it is frightening.

"Manuel, this is incredible. Why is that thing here?"

"You see, Earth is a difficult place, a testing ground. We have wars, sickness, many problems. These other planets have none of these problems. When Earth people are ready to give up the fighting and the greed, then they can go to another planet. You may join them, if you wish." He waits for your answer.

What should you do? On the one hand, your job is here and now on this planet, writing about the Mayas. Yet, the chance to go to another planet may never come again.

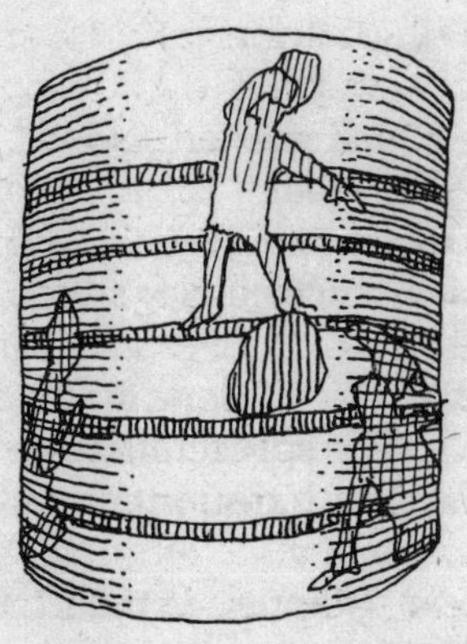

If you decide to go, knowing the danger of never returning, turn to page 27.

If you decide to stay and finish your job, turn to page 28.

You stumble several times as you run down the steps in your escape from the bloodthirsty priests.

"Capture her, kill her," they scream to the warriors in the courtyard. "Don't let her escape!"

Suddenly, a door in the stone steps swings open to reveal a young woman dressed in bright green with yellow beads about her throat.

"I am Camilla, a friend of Manuel, and I will help you. Follow me."

You enter a dark, musty tunnel that slants down from the pyramid.

"Hey, what's going on?"

"Manuel is the head of a secret group that opposes the priests. We want to stop the sacrifice and throw out the priests."

"Where are we going?"

"Kabah. It is a town not too far from here. There you will be hidden at the old temple."

It takes the remainder of the day and the night to get to Kabah. Your feet are sore and blistered by nightfall. But you are so amazed at the beauty of Kabah that you forget how tired you feel. The main temple is covered with carvings of the rain god, Chac. Camilla hides you in a dark room where you are fed a meal of maize, squash, hot chili pepper, and a fermented mead drink. At last you can rest. But fear remains with you, for wherever you go, death lurks.

Go on to the next page.

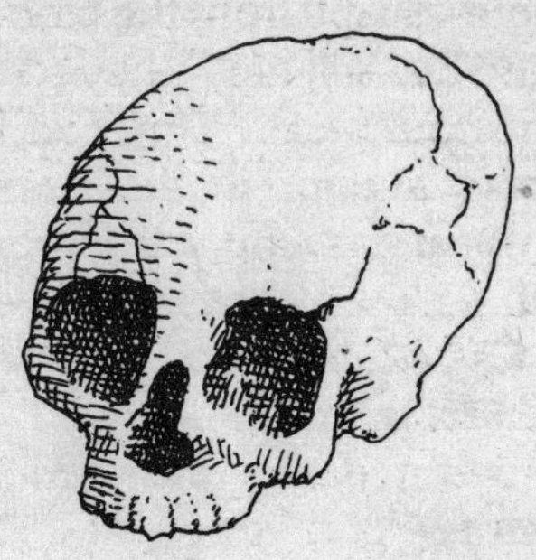

The next day an old man comes and sits before you. With a start you recognize Dr. Lopez from the university.

"My friend, you now see part of the reason for the collapse of the Mayas: evil priests, fear, death."

"But what now, Dr. Lopez?"

"Well, you can stay in Kabah for a while, and live and work as a farmer. Or we can send you to Cozumel, an island off the coast. The journey to the island will be dangerous, but once you are there, the priests will not find you. Here at Kabah you are fairly safe as long as you do what we say. Camilla will help you here."

If you stay in Kabah, turn to page 31.

If you continue the escape to the island, turn to page 33.

You stare at the priests in front of you. Two of them glare at you. One of them fingers his knife, and suddenly you are frightened.

The head priest smiles at you, and says, "Be calm, we will not hurt you. Look in the heavens. There is Venus. It is both the morning and evening star. Venus will guide you as it guides us. Stay with us and learn about the secrets of the universe. Learn of heaven and hell, learn of the power of the four corners of the earth."

You hesitate but decide to stay with this group of people. Three of the priests move forward suddenly and grasp your arms. They shove you toward the blood-spattered altar. Are they going to sacrifice you? One of them speaks.

"You must make a sacrifice to seal your pact with us. There is no turning back. Here is the knife. You will cut out the heart of the victim."

You are horrified. What is to be sacrificed? Is it an animal or a human, some poor slave or prisoner from a battle? If you say you won't do it, will they sacrifice *you?*

If you agree to perform a sacrifice, turn to page 34.

If you refuse, turn to page 36.

You want to see action. But are you prepared to fight? It's one thing to travel in time; it's quite something else to be a warrior involved in real fighting. You could never kill anybody. What if you have to defend yourself?

After three weeks of training, the warrior chief says, "OK, now it is time. You will go on a raid to Itxal, three days from here."

The going is rough, and you and the warriors must travel fast and quietly. Finally, you arrive at the cluster of mud and stick huts that surround a small temple. You all hide in the scrubby bushes waiting for nightfall.

Then, with a bloodthirsty yell, your band leaps from its hiding place and rushes into the open, firing arrows and throwing spears.

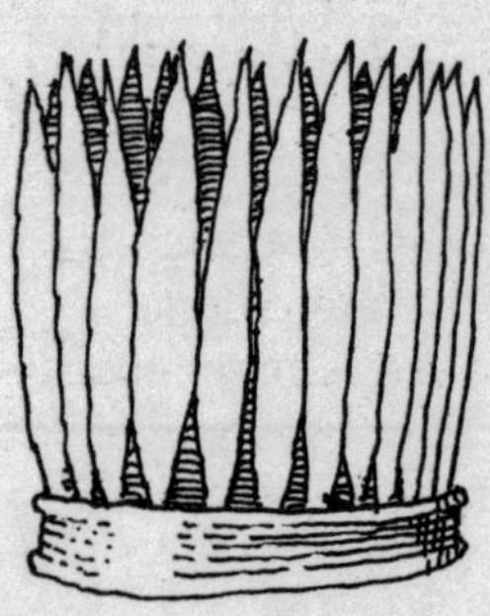

If you join in the fighting, turn to page 37.

If you watch from the hiding place, turn to page 39.

You stay in Chichen Itza. The days are pleasant and you make good friends among the young Mayan warriors.

Some of the people tend the fields while others work making cotton cloth for trading with other Mayan centers. People come to Chichen Itza for great ceremonies, to trade, and to have their disputes settled by the elders.

The Mayas are farmers, traders, and craftsmen. Settlements of houses spread out from Chichen Itza and Uxmal. In this crowded land, water is scarce.

Go on to page 24.

Several of the warriors come together one day. A tall man with broad shoulders speaks, "Would you like to play the ball game?" He explains the game and shows you the court and the hard rubber ball. The game looks fast and difficult. The object is to get the ball through a carved stone hoop. It takes much skill. Teams are made up of eight players. The teams that play in the great ball court on ceremonial days face a real test. If they win, they are heroes; but if they lose, some of them are used as sacrifices in the ceremonies that follow.

You are selected to join one of the teams.

If you refuse to play, turn to page 40.

If you decide to play, turn to page 41.

The words "Temple of the Magicians" excite you. You walk toward the huge pyramid, but a crowd of tourists is busy snapping cameras and pushing and shoving. They surround the base.

You stand for a moment waiting for the crowd to clear, and an old man with wrinkled skin wearing the colorful shawl of the Mayas shuffles up to you.

"Come with me." He beckons with a hand crippled with age.

"I will take you to see a very deep water hole, a secret *cenote*. Water is scarce in this dry land and the *cenotes* are the most important reasons for choosing a place to live. Without water, there is no chance to live. You will be amazed at what I will show you at this *cenote*.

You look around, but Manuel is nowhere to be seen. Where has he gone?

If you go with the old man, turn to page 43.

If you refuse and decide to wait for Manuel, turn to page 44.

The building called the Nunnery is intricately designed with carvings of birds, snakes, and humanlike creatures. No one knows just what the building was used for. The rooms are too dark to have been living quarters. Maybe it was a school building or meeting rooms for the priest and rulers. No one knows.

Poking around in a dark room with a flashlight, you see a piece of white paper stuck to the far wall. It says:

You puzzle over the note. It is Thursday. Is this note for you? How could it be? What should you do?

If you decide to go to the Hotel Maya, turn to page 45.

If you ignore the note and go on to another room, turn to page 46.

One by one, the group standing at the pyramid enters the spacecraft by the transporter beam. Halfway to the spacecraft, their bodies begin to glow. No one seems to be afraid.

Gaining confidence, you step into the transporter beam and are carried up into the spacecraft. No sounds are heard, as you shoot up and away into the far reaches of the universe, to the planet Merganatic. Your quest is over. The true answer to the mystery of the Mayas is here in the spacecraft. The Mayas left the earth because it had become too dangerous a place to live. You are one of the people chosen to escape and start again. What a chance!

The End

You laugh out loud and point at the spacecraft and the people entering it.

"Great show, Manuel, great show! Tell me, how did you do it? What is it, the set for some movie?"

Manuel does not smile and does not speak. He shakes his head and moves off to join the group of people who are going up the transporter beam into the spacecraft.

Go on to page 30.

Then Manuel turns to you; he motions with a small rod that has a beam of light coming from it. Suddenly you are so frightened that the hair on the back of your neck stands up and goose bumps appear on your arms. The beam of light is like an eraser, and it wipes your mind clear of all memory of the day. Then the spacecraft is gone and you are standing at the foot of El Castillo. You can't remember anything that happened after your breakfast with Manuel. It is quiet in the great courtyard. Your big chance has come and gone. You blew it.

The End

You decide to stay in Kabah. The old man whom you recognized as Dr. Lopez invites you to live in his small hut made of clay with a thatched roof. You accept.

That evening Lopez explains to you how the people live.

"The land here is not very good for farming. There is not much water. We cut down the jungle, burn the brush, and then we can plant in the earth."

"But there is so little jungle here. What happened to it?" you ask.

"After six or seven years, the sun dries the earth and the plants take the minerals and nutrients from the soil. The plants won't grow. We must start again and cut more jungle and burn the brush again. The land we leave gets hard and unworkable. This has been going on for hundreds of years."

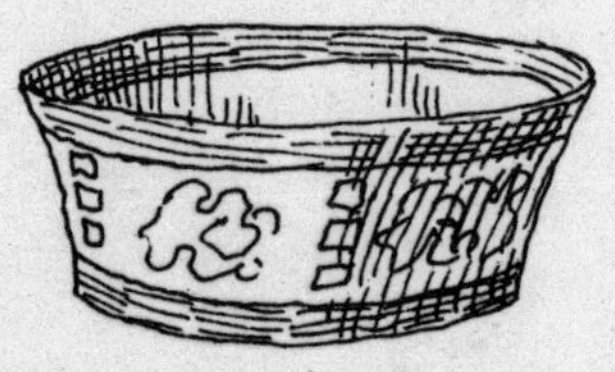

Go on to page 32.

You listen to him and take notes in your brown notebook. He smiles at your attention to detail.

"The people worship the rain god, Chac. He has been good to them, but one day perhaps he will not be, and then the crops will fail."

"What other gods are there?"

"Oh, Plumed Serpent, the ruler of all, and Smoking Mirror, the god of wrath. And there are others too."

You thank Lopez for his kindness and guidance. But after several months working as a farmer you wonder whether you should go on, see more. Yet, Kabah is the center for the group opposing the priests. It's up to you.

If you stay at Kabah, turn to page 47.

If you leave for the coast and pursue the life of a seafaring trader, turn to page 49.

You choose to travel to the coast and the island of Cozumel. Both Dr. Lopez and Camilla tell you of the great beauty of this jewel in the ocean. They describe the clear water and the white beaches and the excitement of the seafaring life.

For more than ten days you walk through the jungle with Camilla. Thorns and dry branches scratch you. Poisonous snakes are a constant danger, the sound of their rattles the only warning. Occasional glimpses of jaguars frighten you even more. But then the jungle thins and turns to sparse grasslands. The smell of the ocean fills the air.

You stand on the shore, feet in the water, letting the sand run through your toes. At a small fishing village you arrange to be taken out by boat to Cozumel. That afternoon you set out.

A sudden squall hits. Great waves crack against the small boat. It fills with water and begins to sink. Salt water fills your mouth, and a strange thing happens. The salt water washes away the effects of the magic potion!

You find yourself in the present again. You have forgotten all about your visit to Dr. Lopez and your trip to the past.

Turn to page 11.

"Yes, I will perform the sacrifice," you whisper. You realize that you are speaking the ancient Mayan tongue.

"Speak up, we can't hear you," the priest with the knife yells at you.

"Yes, I will do a sacrifice, but what for?" You try to hide your fear, but you can't. You tremble and turn quite pale.

The priests look astonished because you have asked this question. They huddle together, talking. The head priest steps forward and says to you, "We make sacrifices to please the gods. Water is scarce, so we sacrifice to the god, Chac, for rain. Crops die in the fields, sickness takes our people. War ruins us. Each time we sacrifice, we hope the gods will treat us better and keep us from harm."

"But," you say, "what can killing someone or something do? I mean, it's crazy. The gods can't want you to kill." You speak without worrying about what the priests will think.

Go on to the next page.

They stare at you. One pushes forward. His eyes flash.

"No more talk. Act. Take the knife. Bring the sacrifice to Chac." The priestess points to the altar.

A slave holding a chicken climbs the temple steps. Behind him two soldiers lead a prisoner kicking and screaming. Looking into the prisoner's eyes, you see the fear of death and the pleading to be saved.

What can you do?

If you accept the knife, turn to page 50.

If you stall for time, turn to page 53.

"No!" you shout, "I will never sacrifice to any god for any reason. You are all crazy."

It was a mistake to say that. The priests become very quiet and solemn. The sun is bright in the sky. Manuel is nowhere to be seen. The sound of a bird breaks the quiet. Two of the priests move toward you. They are not smiling. One says, "Since you will not perform the sacrifice, we will. You will be the victim."

The End

Your attack is a complete success. The element of surprise worked very well. Your band had the upper hand from the first. Even the chickens and dogs belonging to the villagers ran for cover. Dust rose as you raced around. A large group of people led by a woman escaped into the surrounding jungle, but you and your band let them go. You could chase them through underbrush, but it would be too difficult.

Your attempt to take prisoners was not very successful, but you return triumphant, happy that no one was killed or hurt. Manuel welcomes you and says, "So, you like leading the life of a Maya. Well I'm not surprised. Write well when you return to modern times. Write about all you have seen and done."

The End

You watch the fighting from behind a bush. Off to the right you see three of the enemy pulling on a large hemp rope. It releases a bent tree. The tree has a bucket filled with rocks that shower down on you.

"Watch out. Duck!"

Two of your warriors are knocked out. A flurry of arrows and spears fills the air. Three more of your warriors are wounded. Shouts and screams pierce the air. People are running in all directions.

"Retreat. Retreat. Get away!" It is the captain of your group.

The attack is a complete failure. The enemy had more strength and courage than you ever imagined.

When you try to retreat, you become confused. Where do you go? You are cut off from the other warriors. You have lost your sense of direction.

If you go to the left, turn to page 51.

If you go to the right, turn to page 54.

"I'm not playing that game. Find another sucker. Those are the craziest rules I've ever heard. No way. Win, you win; lose, you die."

Several of the warriors nod in agreement, but most of them like the idea of being heroes if they win. The thought of death doesn't frighten them as much as it does you. Some say that it is considered an honor to be sacrificed to a god. Not for you, though.

Two young warriors named Patula and Zacros suggest a hunt for a jaguar that has been seen near the maize fields. You agree to go.

The day is hot, and the track of the jaguar is hard to follow. By late afternoon you are far from the maize and squash fields. Without your friends, you would be lost. You are almost out of water, and night is coming on. Patula says, "We must split up now. I'll go for water. Zacros, you will track the cat. We will meet back here in four hours."

Zacros turns to you. "What do you want to do?"

If you choose to search for water with Patula, turn to page 56.

If you go with Zacros after the jaguar, turn to page 55.

Before you know it, you are on the field in the ball court. Shouting fills the air as the two teams practice. A large crowd gathers to watch.

Go on to page 42.

Six priests, three elders, and a group dressed in clothes of golden cloth march in, take their honored places, and signal for the game to begin.

You are frightened. What if you lose? Your eyes quickly travel to the steps of the pyramid called El Castillo. You have heard of victims with hearts ripped out being thrown down the steps into the courtyard. You tremble as you imagine it happening to you.

The game is long and hard. The score is close. The other team has one point. Your heart pounds. But then with loud screams and yells, a raiding party bursts into the ball court. They are Toltecs, a tribe of fierce warriors from the north and west of what is now called Mexico. You hide in the bushes next to the big *cenote*. Others are not so lucky and die in agony. The day is over, but you are still alive.

The Toltecs fan out and hunt for survivors. As you try to escape, you are spotted and chased. Your heart pounding, you feel as though life is already over. Then the spear hits you in the middle of the back.

The End

You have always been an adventurer, so of course you follow the old man to the secret *cenote.* The trail is a faint path through the tangle of bushes, and within fifteen minutes you are tired and completely lost.

"Hey, old man, where is this *cenote* of yours?"

He turns and smiles at you.

"Here it is."

But instead of a *cenote,* you find yourself surrounded by three men. One of them holds a gun, the other two have knives. They do not smile.

"Give us your money."

You fumble for your wallet. There are two American ten dollar bills and 300 Mexican pesos. You hand them over to the men. They tie you up with rough hemp rope, load you onto a donkey, and move off into the jungle.

"We will hold you for ransom. Your people will pay and pay plenty. If they don't, you die."

You hope that your friends and your family will be able to come up with the ransom money. You know for sure that your investigation of the Mayan civilization will have to be postponed for a while.

The End

You ignore this crazy old man. He probably wants money and will lead you on a wild goose chase. You don't have time for that.

As you walk away from him, a rock with a piece of paper wrapped around it drops at your feet. You look up, startled, but you see no one who could have dropped this rock.

The paper contains a short message that says:

RETURN TO THE NUNNERY.
MEET WITH US IN
THE SEVENTH ROOM

The message is signed with a red handprint.

What should you do? Manuel is walking back toward you. You rush over and show him the note. Manuel looks at the note and shakes his head.

"Leave it alone. It could be dangerous."

If you decide to ignore Manuel's advice and go to the Nunnery, turn to page 58.

If you decide to ignore the instructions in the note and go instead to the Mexican police, turn to page 57.

Who put the note in the darkened room? Who could have known you would be there and would find it? It might well be the secret forces of the Mayas at work—forces too hidden for most humans to understand. You are fascinated.

You check into the Hotel Maya. At nine o'clock when you walk down the corridor to room 327, soldiers leap out of rooms 328 and 329, and arrest you. They are all heavily armed. You can smell the oil on the weapons. Their captain speaks to you in Spanish, but then switches to English when you don't reply.

"So, you are the spy we have been waiting for. We knew we would catch you. If you are wondering what happened to your friend in room 327, I'll tell you. He was captured two days ago, and is now in jail. You revolutionaries are all the same."

The captain orders the soldiers to take you away to arrest you.

If you plead innocence, turn to page 60.

If you tell the truth, turn to page 59.

Don't like taking chances, do you? OK, go ahead. The next room is small and as dark as the others. You step cautiously into the room. Suddenly the floor beneath you gives way and you fall into a bright blue space, gathering speed at the rate of 32 feet per second. The rush of air against you flattens your nose against your face, slicks your hair back, and squishes your lips. Then with a bump you land in—China.

You can't believe it when you look into the tunnel that dropped you on the other side of the earth. You are standing in a rice paddy with water above your ankles and green rice shoots around your legs.

Four people wearing straw hats, blue cotton pants and shirts run up to you. They yell at you and shout and wave their arms. You want to get away from them, but it is impossible. They tie your arms behind your back and lead you away. Finally two uniformed men come and officially arrest you in the name of the People's Republic.

You will be held in prison as a spy for three years.

The End

Kabah is rich in history and tradition. The rain god Chac adorns the walls of the temples. The Plumed Serpent is carved on most of the buildings. A girl of eleven named Mimla and a boy of fifteen named Ordex become your friends and companions. Daily you work the fields of maize and squash and peppers. In the heat of the day you gather under the shelter of thatched roofs and play the Mayan games of chance and skill called Mara Coo. The old people tell stories and recite poems about glorious leaders, bloody wars, fierce or loving gods. You are careful to watch for the dreaded but honored rattlesnakes, for they lurk in the dry bush ready to kill.

Go on to page 48.

Again you grow restless, and one day you ask Dr. Lopez for permission to leave Kabah and travel either ahead in time in Mayan history or back in time. He listens and is somewhat saddened that you want to leave Kabah.

"If you stay, you could have a brilliant future as a member of our group. Soon we will overthrow the priests. But if you must go, it is alright. When you return to your own land in your own time, write about what really happened to the Mayas. But I know that time grows heavy and you want to go. You choose."

If you decide to go ahead in time,
turn to page 62.

If you decide to go back in time,
turn to page 64.

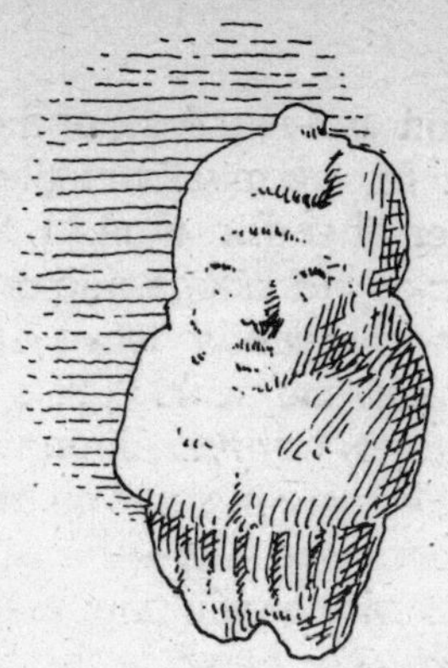

You arrive on the island of Cozumel after four days of travel by boat. Cozumel is a paradise. Coral reefs glimmer in a rainbow of colors. Giant sea turtles swim near the northern end of the island, and birds fill the air at sunrise and sunset. It is hard to tell where the sea ends and the sky begins.

The island is the home of Mayan traders who travel up and down the coast exchanging cloth, jade, fish, and pottery. The people are good seafarers who know the weather and the winds and the ways of the sea. You would like to join them on their cruises.

When you approach the captain of one of the trading ships, he says that there are jobs aboard his ship. He asks if you would like to join an expedition as a sailor.

If you say "Yes," turn to page 65.

If you tell the captain that you don't know how to sail, but that you can do other jobs on board, turn to page 66.

Human sacrifices! Throughout history people have been sacrificed to appease gods. Fortunately, this time it is the chicken that is to be sacrificed. Even so, it is not easy to draw the stone knife across the chicken's throat and watch its lifeblood flow onto the altar.

You decide to try to bring an end to this needless sacrifice. Perhaps if you volunteer to work with the prisoners who are to be sacrificed, you will be able to devise a plan to help them escape. Time is running out, because the ceremony of sacrifice is only three weeks away.

If you plan to escape, turn to page 67.

If you call in Manuel and plead for help, turn to page 68.

You turn left and follow a path that leads away from the clearing. You hope you're going in the right direction. The retreat through the jungle is terrible. At first you feel as though your lungs might burst from running so hard. Then you feel the muscles in your legs begin to tighten. You don't think you can take another step. A root catches your foot, and you fall forward. The last thing you remember is the earth rushing toward you. You black out.

When you come to, you examine your head and arms and legs. Everything is all right except for a bump on your forehead. Your mouth is dry and your tongue feels swollen.

You call out, "Anybody there?" Maybe that's a dumb thing to do. The enemy could be nearby and might hear you.

If you continue to call for help, turn to page 69.

If you decide to lie still and rest while you gather strength, turn to page 70.

The priests wait impatiently as you ramble on about not wanting to kill anyone. Their eyes gleam and their bodies shake as though with fever.

"You must do it," one of them shouts at you. "You must!"

"But it isn't right. I can't kill. I won't kill."

One of the priests lunges at you, but you step to one side. He tumbles down the steps of the temple. The crowd of people standing below look up in horror. In the confusion, you sneak around to the other side and clamber down the steps. Although they are extremely steep, you make it and manage to lose yourself in the crowd. You ask someone where the warriors can be found. He points to the courtyard. You decide to join them. No one can be more warlike than the priests. Perhaps the warriors will be more civilized.

Turn to page 13.

"So, you thought you could escape, did you? Well, you will be punished. You are perfect for our next sacrifice to the rain god." It is the enemy chief talking. You have been captured. You made the wrong turn.

An old priestess with deep wrinkles rushes up and says, "No, we don't need a sacrifice. We need a slave to work for us in the temple. This prisoner will do." Her name is Muscla and she has a great deal of power, for the chief listens to her and agrees.

"Take this pest, do what you wish! We'll catch others."

Later that day you are put into a dark room in the back of a small temple. It smells of wood smoke. As you enter you notice the imprint of a hand—a red hand on the wall. You have read about it but what does it mean?

Then a strange thing begins to happen. Your vision blurs and musical noise fills the air. When you reach out to touch the wall, you feel dizzy and begin to stumble. That's it! The potion is wearing off. You are on your way back to the present.

Turn to page 11.

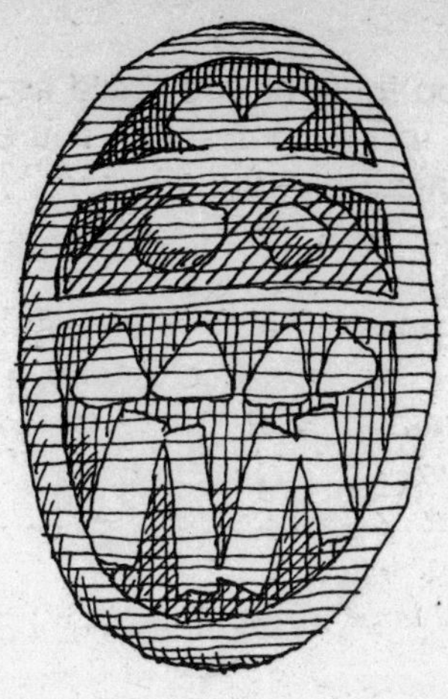

Tracking the jaguar isn't easy. The cat is sly and moves quietly through the bush. You try to guess what its next move will be. Whenever you think the cat is ahead of you, it suddenly appears behind you or off to the side. Maybe the jaguar is tracking *you*. You become so absorbed in this pursuit that you lose all track of time and place. You yell for Zacros, but he's nowhere to be found. You don't know where to go or where to turn. You are lost!

Then you hear sounds of people talking. None of them sounds like Zacros. They might be friends or they might be a band of enemy raiders. You hide behind some bushes and wait and watch. You can't really tell whether they are friends or enemies.

If you ask them for help, turn to page 72.

If you go on by yourself, turn to page 74.

With your friend Patula you follow an old, unused path that winds between low-lying hills and thickets. The path ends abruptly at a *cenote*. You see signs that the path had actually gone down into the *cenote*. "Hey, Patula, what do you think this means?"

"I don't know. Maybe we should investigate." You plunge into the cool, fresh water and swim down toward an opening. It could either be a man-made tunnel or a natural cave. Coming back up for air you tell your companion you have seen glittering gold, jade rings of the deepest green, and plates of silver. Both of you descend, and enter the tunnel. You come out into a huge underground cavern. In the corner of the cavern lies the treasure of gold and jade. It is beautiful beyond your wildest imagination.

"Wow, it's the treasure, the lost treasure of the Plumed Serpent." Patula grabs for the gold.

You stare at this treasure in amazement. You want to claim it.

Do you try to take the gold now? If so, *turn to page 76.*

If you decide to return to modern times to collect this fabulous treasure, *turn to page 77.*

You see two policemen near the tourist buses.

"We're sorry but we can't help you. We are too busy."

You show them the note. When they see the sign of the red hand, they become very excited.

"Wait! Just one minute. Don't leave. Stay right there."

They talk in hushed tones, and then they radio their headquarters.

"The captain is coming right away."

Soon you hear the whining of a helicopter. When it lands in the courtyard, three men get out.

"What's this all about? Let me see the note." It is the captain speaking. He is a fat man with a black mustache.

"Aha! I see. The red hand. You are in trouble. This is the mark of revolutionaries. How did you come by this note? Why do they want you?"

They search you and find your little brown book with the notes you have been taking since the beginning of this trip. The fat man scowls and says. "So, secret notes. Well, well! Come with us."

If you cooperate with the police,
turn to page 78.

If you just want to get out of this mess
of the "red hand," turn to page 79.

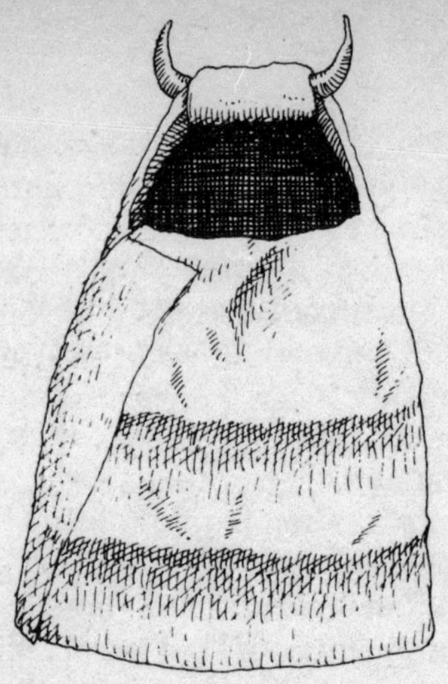

The red handprint is ominous. What can it mean?

You enter the seventh room in the Nunnery building. Although it is dark inside, you see a face. It is luminous, and glows with a soft, yellowish light. A person clothed in silver with golden arm bands and a clear helmet stands in the middle of the room.

"Earthling, the age of destruction is near. You are chosen as a survivor. If you wish, you can leave the earth with us four days from now."

You listen in amazement to all that he says. Is the world really coming to an end? It sounds like the prediction made by Mayan priests hundreds and hundreds of years ago. It is scary, because maybe they were right.

Manuel suddenly appears. "Go with them. It is time."

You go with them.

The End

"But Captain, this is all a mistake. I am a writer investigating the Mayan civilization. I'm no spy."

The captain leads you into a room where three men are seated at a table. They look up when you enter. The thin one says, "Wrong person! Who is this? That's not the one we want."

The man says, "Let the prisoner go. We are just wasting valuable time. The spy has had warning and time to escape. As for you, stay out of trouble."

You leave the room shaking with excitement and relief.

Since you have left Uxmal, you might as well go on and examine the ruins of Chichen Itza.

Turn to page 16.

"Captain, it's all a mistake. I was on my way to my own room. I just came to this room by mistake. I'm no revolutionary or spy. You must believe me."

The captain laughs, "They all say that. You are all the same. Spies, radicals, thieves. We have a way to deal with you!"

You are handcuffed, put into a jeep and driven to Merida. There you are thrown into a small, damp, evil-smelling cell in the local jail. The captain comes to see you the next day to tell you that the judge has given you a thirty year sentence for plotting to overthrow the government.

"But I've had no trial," you protest.

"We caught you red-handed, and we don't believe in trials anyway. These are dangerous times."

He stubs out a cigarette in the earthen floor, sticks his short, brown hands in his pockets, and walks away from your cell. You grab the bars of the cell and scream for help. Three guards at the end of the corridor just laugh. Face it! You will be in jail for a long time.

The End

You want to go ahead at least one hundred years. ZAP! You are standing in the same spot but you notice a great change. The earth has become hard from overuse. Plants can't grow. The fields are sun-scorched and brown.

The few people stare at you. They are thin and their eyes are empty looking. No one smiles. No one greets you. There is no noise, only the sound of wind blowing in the dry bushes around the huts that were once filled with people. There are only a few children and they, too, are quiet and appear unhappy. It is a sad sight.

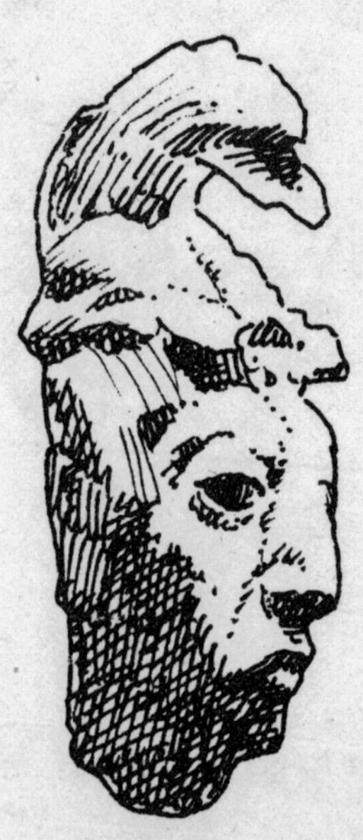

Dr. Lopez stands beside you. He does not smile; sadness fills his face.

"You see, the rains did not come. The earth was worn out. The crops died in the sun. You have witnessed one of the reasons for the collapse of the Mayas."

You nod your head solemnly before you begin to scribble notes in the brown book.

Where to next? Lopez says you can leave Kabah and travel on a southwesterly course to the hills and lush rain forests. Or you can follow the trail that leads back to Uxmal.

If you want to go to the hills and rain forests, turn to page 82.

If you want to go to Uxmal, turn to page 80.

You take a sip from the bottle of time potion you've been carrying since you left Dr. Lopez's study. Then . . .

Huge raindrops smash onto the surface of the earth. The sky is completely covered with heavy clouds. The rain has been falling for millions of years. A mist rises off rocks and is carried away by winds of gale force.

Something went wrong with the time change! You have gone back too far into the past, several billion years back to a time when rain fell and earth was a spinning ball in the universe, gradually cooling. All is dark, for the clouds block the sun. You have gone back to the beginning of the world.

You stand there drenched in the downpour. You are alone. You scream out, "What do I do now?" It is useless, for there is no one on earth at this time. Then a voice at once familiar to you says, *"You still have some of the magic potion. Drink it,"* Manuel commands.

If you take a sip of what's left,
turn to page 83.

If you drink every drop of the potion,
turn to page 84.

You have been a sailor almost all of your life. The sea is like a second home to you. The ship the Mayas use is not what you are used to, but sailing is the same all over.

"Come along, then. We are leaving right away." It is the captain speaking.

You are told to cast off. Later that day, as the boat cuts through the water, you see black storm clouds gathering to the east.

"Captain, looks like a blow coming."

"The storms here are fierce." Suddenly the water is savage. "It looks bad."

All crew members are alerted. But the storm breaks fast. Vicious waves pound the hull, and gale-force winds rip at the sail. The waves try to wrench the tiller from your hands. The rough water stings your eyes and drenches your clothes.

The captain asks *you* for advice.

If you suggest he continue on course, turn to page 85.

If you suggest finding land, turn to page 86.

"No, I'm not a sailor, but I learn fast, and I'll work hard. I love the sea." You hope the captain will take you on.

The captain looks you over carefully. He thinks for a short while, and then he says, "I'll try you out. Watch the others closely and do what you're told." He walks over to talk with two people who stand on the dock. They are merchants who want the captain to take their cargo to a village up the coast.

The captain talks for some minutes, then he waves you over.

"Go with these men. Bring back the cargo. Hurry."

You walk up a steep, sandy path to three large huts. Stored in the huts are turtle shells, yellow and red cloth, carved wooden figures, dried fish, and pottery. The Mayas trade goods rather than use money.

One of the men says to you, "We need someone around here full time to help. Why not stay with us?"

"Where will I live?"

"We'll fix that. You can live in one of our houses."

If you decide to stay on the island,
turn to page 87.

If you decide to go back to the ship,
turn to page 88.

Escape from the temple is a problem. Guards are alert to any noise or movement. But the warrior prisoners know that this is their one chance. Together, you wait until nightfall. Only the sound of insects fills the air. Then you creep forward, overpower two guards, rush down the temple steps and spread out into the darkened courtyard of the temple.

The escape is a success! The guards were easy to overpower. Maybe they don't really believe in sacrifices either. Could it be that only the priests want the sacrifices in order to control the people by fear?

If you try to raise a revolt against the priests, turn to page 91.

If you decide that it is time to escape once and for all and get back to modern times, turn to page 92.

"Manuel, help! I didn't bargain for this."

Once again your mysterious friend appears.

"Choose the right hand or the left hand." He holds out his clenched fists for you to make your choice.

"What kind of a choice is that, Manuel? I mean, that's just like rolling dice."

Manuel looks at you long and hard. His black eyes almost burn through you.

"The choices lie deep within you. Do not hesitate. Choose now."

If you point to the right hand, turn to page 93.

If you choose the left, turn to page 94.

Your cries for help have been heard by two of your warriors. They are at your side now and help you to your feet. You are groggy, but with their help you stumble on through the jungle for more than three hours. The cries of your pursuers grow fainter.

Finally you are able to stop and rest, hidden by a small rock outcropping. One of the warriors cleans the cut on your forehead and squeezes the juices from a plant into the wound.

The three of you rest for the night, taking turns keeping a watchful eye on the surrounding jungle.

When the orange sun finally appears in the sky, you all give thanks and continue back to Chichen Itza. "My friends, without you, I would be lost. I owe my life to you."

It wasn't a successful raid, but at least you got back alive.

The End

You lie on the ground feeling dizzy and sick to your stomach. The earth spins around and the colors you see are a blur. You grip a rock in your right hand, trying to hold on. Then you faint.

When you waken, you are cold, hungry, stiff and alone. The call of an owl echoes in the jungle. Sounds of twigs snapping and dry leaves rustling seem louder than they would if you weren't frightened.

Then two people appear, creeping from tree to tree. You hold your breath and don't move a muscle. They are coming toward you. You can almost feel one of their spears pushing into your back.

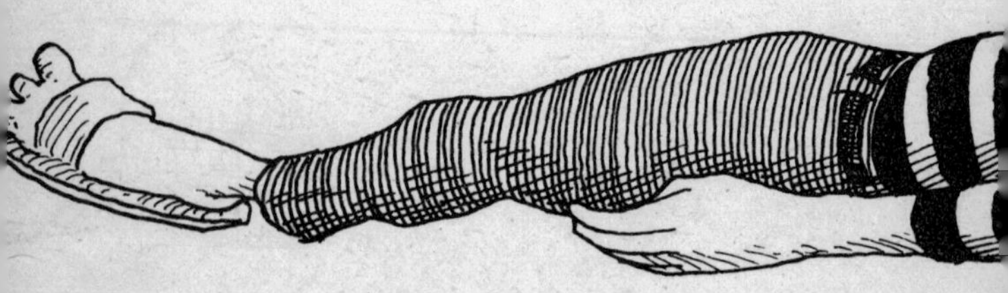

As they get closer, you realize that the only things they are carrying in their hands are—cameras! They have been creeping around to take pictures of the rare birds in the area. Your time potion has worn off. You must have been out cold for a whole day.

Soon you are being rushed to the hospital. As you lean back in the ambulance, you smile weakly at these two kind people who have rescued you. You don't bother starting the story of your time travel. You know they'll never believe you.

The End

You don't know who these people are or where they have come from, but talking to them is worth the risk. You couldn't survive long in this desolate area alone without food and water. You sneak toward them through the jungle fearful of making even the slightest noise. The talking grows louder.

Peering around a clump of bushes, you see a group of men seated around a small fire. They are eating. The food smells good and you are very hungry. You step out from behind the tree. Before you have a chance to say anything, the men jump to their feet. Several grab their short spears. They surround you.

"Hey, I'm friendly. I'm not an enemy. I'm lost."

The leader shouts commands.

Go on to the next page.

"Tie the prisoner up. Quick!"

Rough hemp rope binds your arms and legs. You are suddenly pushed to the ground. The rope bites at your wrists.

"Where are you from? Tell us or you die."

"I'm from Chichen Itza." You try to hide your trembling.

The leader smiles an evil smile.

"We are Toltecs. You Mayas are fools. We will conquer you. Now, lead us to your city."

"I'm lost."

"Liar! Lead us to Chichen Itza and maybe you'll go free. If you don't we'll send you back north to Teotihuacan with the other prisoners. He points at a sullen group of Mayas who are tied up just as you are. You recognize Zacros among them.

If you agree to try to lead them to Chichen Itza, turn to page 96.

If you refuse, turn to page 95.

You wait quietly in the bushes for more than an hour. Finally the voices fade until you no longer hear them. You peer around a clump of trees. You see about fifty people surrounding a giant spaceship. It is at least one hundred feet high. Huge fins stick out from the side, portholes dot the entire length. It is as shiny as a mirror. A huge landing ramp projects from the middle section. Several small saucer-shaped craft rest on the ramp. You can hardly believe your eyes, but it *is* real.

The people are wearing silver suits with orange stripes on the arms and legs. One group of ten or so is working on the saucer ships. Another group appears to be removing water from the main ship. Still another group is studying large maps and charts that are suspended in air! You can just make them out. Some look like maps of the constellations in the Milky Way; others look like galaxies unknown to you. The maps are like circuit boards, and lights flash along routes from star to star.

Go on to the next page.

You hear someone speaking.

"Soon. The time has come. We must leave by nightfall. The stars are in the right position for our leap into outer space."

Another says, "But have we assembled all the people? Let's not just hurry."

You start to move forward. Strangely you are not afraid. They haven't seen you yet. You stop to think about it for a few minutes. Now you must decide.

If you announce your presence,
turn to page 98.

If you go back into the protection of the jungle and hope to find Zacros, turn to page 99.

The lure of gold is great. From the beginning of time, people have worshipped the shiny metal. They have fought wars, plundered cities, murdered in its name. Some say gold has a curse on it.

You lose all track of time and place. You seat yourself in front of the treasure and feel the smooth metal. Time passes quickly, until a rumbling sound wakens you from your dreams of wealth. Rocks tumble from the roof of the cavern; boulders slide down and seal off the cave. The air grows hot. Soon the oxygen will be gone.

You are finished. Greed has gotten the best of you.

The End

Leaving Patula, you run as fast as you can out of the cave, and along the path back to Chichen Itza where you find Manuel.

"Manuel, Manuel, I want to go back to modern times. Please send me back."

Manuel studies your face. He does not smile.

"If that is your wish, it will be done. But don't be hasty."

"I want to go."

Suddenly you are in the present time, driving out to see if you can find the *cenote* where the gold is. A modern road has been built over the old path. When you reach the site, you park the car. Trembling with excitement, you put on a wet suit and aqualung and dive below the surface of the *cenote*.

To your horror the entrance to the cave has been almost completely blocked by a landslide. It looks like there is barely enough room for you to get in. But if you were to go for help, others will know about your discovery.

If you try to enter the cave through the small hole in the landslide, turn to page 100.

If you decide to return to the surface and go for help, turn to page 101.

You are taken to police headquarters in the captain's helicopter. For hours you repeat your story. The police keep firing questions at you.

"How did you get here?"

"Why did you come here?"

"Tell us the truth."

Finally they give up the questioning. Everyone is exhausted. The captain now turns to you, snubs out his evil-smelling cigarette in the full ashtray, looks you in the eye and says, "OK." He pauses. "Are you brave? Will you agree to become a double agent? Join the revolutionary gang. Pretend to be one of them. We need information. You can help us stop this revolt."

"But how can I do it? They'll find out that I'm working for you and they'll kill me."

"That is the risk you take, but what can I say? We need help."

"Where would I start if I agree to be a double agent."

The captain points to a map on the wall. "See, there is the island of Cozumel. It is a hotbed of revolutionaries. You would go there. Or you could go to Merida. That is the headquarters of the gang."

If you agree and want to go to Merida,
turn to page 102.

If you agree to go to Cozumel,
turn to page 103.

You start to run but soon you are surrounded by angry policemen. Manuel comes up to you and whispers in your ear, "If you take this time potion now you'll get out of this mess. Here."

He hands you a small bottle and you drink it. The police are amazed because one moment you are there and the next you are gone.

"What happened? Where, where, where did the prisoner go?"

It's too late. You are back in the past. They will never find you.

The End

At Uxmal the jungle has covered the stone buildings. You see the mounds of green bushes and shrubs, and you realize that underneath the bushes are the temples and houses. It's fascinating to you that this same place was once so prosperous, filled with happy people. Now centuries later it is a desolate ghost town. No sounds are heard.

You take out your notebook and compare

what you've seen of the past to what you see now. It is going to be difficult to write a book about all this, but that is your job.

Two people approach you from the edge of the jungle. Wow! It's Manuel and a friend.

"You see, the rains stopped. No crops grew. The people believed that Chac, the rain god, grew angry with them."

"What happened then? From the looks of the jungle the rains must have come back."

Manuel answers, "Oh, they did. But by that time the people had moved on, searching for better land and more water. The people believed that Chac had cursed the area."

"What about the priests? Couldn't they stop the people from moving away."

Manuel says, "No, in fact they went with them, or at least most did. Have you seen enough?"

You are not satisfied. Drought can destroy a civilization, but you somehow feel that this was not the only factor.

Start your investigation over again.
Go back to page 11.

You have heard people speak of the hill country to the south. They tell stories of a great rain forest, large temples, pyramids and rich soil. They also speak of warfare with those from the west who raid the towns in search of prisoners and treasure.

You set out with a guide toward the fabled hills in the south.

For days you travel under the blistering sun. Water is scarce, and your food runs out. After a while you begin to doubt that your guide knows where he is going. You wish you knew more about astronomy so that you could use the stars to guide the way; but you don't, nor does your guide. You grow weaker and weaker from lack of food and water. After almost eight days you can barely walk. You must have some water. But there is none.

You are never seen or heard from again.

The End

Your time skip works well this time. It leads you forward from the beginning of time to the year 16,000 BC. There are no Mayas. There are no temples or stone buildings of any sort. You see a group of twenty or thirty people. But strangely they can't see or hear you. You are invisible to them. You can only observe.

For three months you travel with these people, invisible all the while. They hunt in small groups of two and three. The young children are taken care of by the older people. The older children help in gathering wild grains and berries and roots. These people don't live in permanent huts. They are constantly breaking camp and moving on to better land richer with game.

Then one day, one of the people suddenly points to you and screams.

"Ah, agha, yah, yah."

"Match, yagah, utoo."

They pick up spears and clubs. You are no longer invisible. But you make a sign of peace by holding your arms wide open and smiling. They stop shouting and cautiously approach you.

Suppose you were to stay and teach them what you know about the future of mankind. Would history be changed?

If you stay and try to teach these people, turn to page 112.

If you want to leave this time slot and go to a Mayan time, turn to page 113.

ZONK! You really skipped ahead this time. You accelerated past the present time and into the distant future. You have come four billion years ahead of where you were. The earth has become a frozen planet bathed in darkness, slowly turning in the void. The sun has burned itself out. Messages from outer space reach you on a microreceiver that was mysteriously given to you in your zoom forward.

Some of the messages are SOS calls from Venus, others are from Mars, and still others are from planets in distant galaxies. But the message repeats itself and begins to call your very own name. It says, "We are your friends. We will help you get away from Earth. Earth is finished. Wait for us."

Of course, there is nothing you can do but wait anyway.

You are picked up by a team of space creatures who want you to visit either the Planet of Dreams or the Region of Light.

The space creatures transmit a message from Dr. Lopez. It says that the Planet of Dreams might answer all your hopes; the Region of Light will help you help others.

If you go to the Planet of Dreams,
turn to page 116.

If you go to the Region of Light,
go to page 114.

The captain decides to maintain his course, but the storm shifts direction. Gale-force winds and huge waves force your ship in an easterly direction. It is all you can do to keep the ship from swamping. One sailor is swept overboard, his screams lost in the roar of the waves.

"Captain, can't you do anything?" you scream in despair.

He does not answer, for all his attention is given to the sea and the wind.

For a whole day, your boat is tossed about by the waves. Then, once again, the wind picks up in force. You are propelled like a motorboat.

"Land! Land straight ahead," a lookout shouts. Then you all see it. Palm trees, white beaches, high mountains. You have reached what someday will be called Cuba. The boat slams through the surf and grates to rest on the beach. You are met by a group of Arawak Indians. They are friendly and offer rest and food. They are tall and bronze, with broad smiling faces. They invite you to stay with them.

If you choose to stay in Cuba, turn to page 104.

If you continue with the ship back to Cozumel and the trade route, turn to page 105.

The captain decides to head for home port. Just as you come about and run with the wind for the island of Cozumel, a squall hits and cracks the mast. The boat founders; the rudder is useless.

Helpless, you watch as wave after wave batters the boat, until finally one enormous wave, four times the size of the others, sweeps over the frail craft. With a wrenching crash, the boat breaks up.

You hold onto a piece of mast. It serves as a float, and after four hours you are washed ashore. You are the lone survivor. Enough of the sailor's life for you.

Gasping for breath, you call out to Manuel and ask him to bring you back into the present.

"What is it, my friend?" It is the voice of Manuel.

"I want out. I've had enough."

"Your wish is granted."

Suddenly you are back in Merida. Was it all a dream? When you look in your brown notebook, it is full of writing.

You have more than enough information to write a book.

The End

You work in the hot, musty storage sheds, stacking wicker baskets and keeping accurate count of what comes in and what goes out. Trading ships come to the harbor every day. Small, narrow sailboats crowd the docks.

You are concerned with reports that a terrible sickness is wiping out whole villages along the coast. One ship reported that in a town two days away, most of the people have become ill and many of them have died. You question a sailor from the ship.

"What's the sickness like?" you ask.

The sailor pauses, then replies, "Well, people run high fevers. They rave and shiver, and then fall quiet. Sometimes they are dead the same day. It's horrible. The gods must be angry."

He seems to be describing a plague. No one knows where the germs come from. Perhaps there are rats on the trading ships. With no drug to combat it, the plague could wipe everybody out. What can you do? You are frightened. You could be the next victim.

If you try to organize a medical team, turn to page 106.

If you decide to leave the island, turn to page 107.

The work on board ship is hard, but you are learning about the Mayas as you sail from town to town. They are talented potters. They weave beautiful cloth of orange and gold and brown. They carve figures of their gods. Theirs is a rich and varied culture.

Go on to page 90.

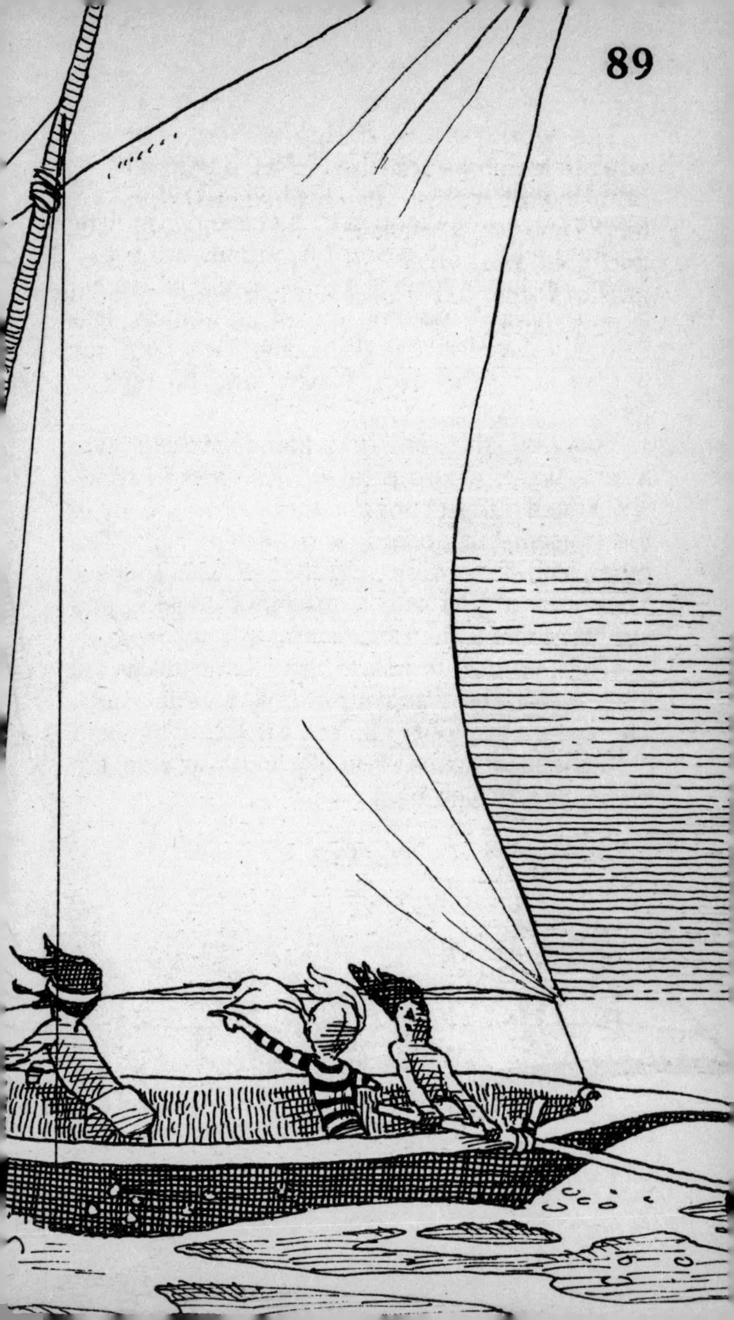

Then one day, a strange thing happens. Just as you are putting out to sea, the lookout shouts, "A mountain, a white mountain, a volcano is moving on the water." He waves and shouts frantically. There on the horizon is a large, white passenger liner. Smoke is pouring out of its funnels. It is flying the Swedish flag. As it comes closer you see people lining the deck, waving and taking pictures.

You, your ship, and your friends are caught in a time warp, where parallel lines cross in space and time flip-flops back and forth. Now you are in the present but aboard your ancient craft! The other ship is a cruise ship loaded with tourists. They look at you with amusement thinking you are just some local fishermen in a funny boat.

When you try to talk to them your voices fall into a void. The time warp is only a visual warp. There is no way out of it. You are locked in fixed time in fixed space. For eternity you ride the waves in a Mayan boat.

The End

Where do you begin? How do you start a revolt? It sounds great, but the priests are powerful. They have spies everywhere, and they are suspicious of everyone and everything. Their suspicions grow out of their greedy and evil ways. Suspected revolutionaries are quickly dragged up to a sacrificial altar and their hearts are ripped out. The people tremble in fear of this group of priests. Probably time will overcome the priests. They will grow lazy and contented. Then revolts will happen and justice will prevail.

Now it's time for you to return to the present and write about what you have learned.

The End

You are very frightened. You must get out of this place fast! Suddenly you are back in Merida watching television in your hotel room. Your decision for the night is where to go out and have dinner.

The End

Slowly, Manuel unclenches his right fist. Inside it is a key to a safe-deposit box at the Merida airport. He smiles and says, "You are on your way, my friend. The trip is over. You are back in the present. There is a gift for you in the safe-deposit box."

"What do you mean, Manuel? I've barely gotten started. I need to find out more." You search his face, but you see nothing, no anger, no fear, no worry.

"It is time to go. Good-bye."

When you reach the airport, you open the box with the key. In it is a note. It says:

> THE PLUMED SERPENT,
> THE MOST POWERFUL GOD
> OF THE MAYAS, WISHES YOU
> LUCK. GO BACK WHERE YOU
> CAME FROM AND STUDY YOUR
> OWN COUNTRY. MAYBE YOU
> CAN HELP YOUR PEOPLE.
> THEY ARE IN DANGER.

In the box is a gold figure of a snake with feathers near its head. It is small, carved with great detail, and its golden color gleams.

The End

The left hand opens slowly revealing a small clay figure. It is a good luck charm from Manuel to you. It is his way of saying that you will be successful in your life, no matter what you choose to do. It makes you feel happy and secure to hold this small clay figure.

"Thank you, Manuel. You have been a good guide." You smile and Manuel smiles back. Then an amazing thing happens! There is a puff of purple smoke and Manuel vanishes. You stare at the spot where he was standing just a second before. On the floor is a bright green feather, small and stiff.

Your trip is over.

The End

You give in to the Toltecs. After all, you couldn't find your way back to Chichen Itza if you tried. The trail back to Teotihuacan is long and hot. You and Zacros and the twelve other prisoners are guarded by three Toltecs. The marches are hard, starting right before sunrise when the sky lightens. Through the hot day the pace never slackens. Food is scarce and you are all hungry. Night is a welcome relief from the forced march, and sleep comes easily.

You follow a route that avoids settlements, but there seems to be no hope of escape. The guards are watchful, but they are not cruel. Finally, you arrive at the huge city, Teotihuacan, and the Temple of the Sun and the Moon. It is a magnificent city surrounded by mountains. Around the huge temple pyramids connected by the Highway of the Dead are buildings that look like modern apartment towers.

You are thrown in with another group of prisoners and questioned by three Toltecs.

"Where did you come from? Who are you? What are you after? What is the small brown thing you carry with the white leaves in it?" You answer as best you can, but they don't really believe or understand you. They offer you a choice by holding a fistful of straws. The bottom of each straw has been dipped in red, blue or yellow dye. You close your eyes and pick a straw.

If you draw a red one, turn to page 127.

If you draw a blue one, turn to page 128.

If you draw a yellow one, turn to page 132.

What a bind you are in!

Guiding a Toltec raiding party going to Chichen Itza is dangerous, because if you are captured by Mayas you will be accused of being a traitor. If that doesn't happen, you will be thrown in with the Toltecs. Yet, your chances for escaping from the Toltecs seems better if you find Chichen Itza. If only you had some help!

Stepping over a tree trunk, you lift your leg high. Without even a rattle for a warning, a large snake strikes. The fangs sink deep into your leg. The eyes of the beast glare at you. You begin to faint, but then the snake turns into a feathered bird! It is the Plumed Serpent—mystical god of the Mayas. In a deep tone of command the Serpent tells you that he has chosen you as the new leader of the people.

With courage and pride you step forward. You seem a foot taller than before. Your eyes shine with power. The Toltecs fall down and tremble with fear.

If you accept this royal privilege, turn to page 129.

If you see this as an opportunity to escape the Toltecs, turn to page 130.

As you step from behind the bushes, you cross a sensor beam. It warns of your presence. People look up and wave at you. They are not surprised or even frightened that you are there.

A young woman steps forward to address you. Her name is Cruzora.

"Welcome. It is good to have you with us. Nothing really happens by chance. You were destined to join us."

She is friendly and you take an immediate liking to her. The others, too, greet you with smiles and waves. All are busy at one project or another. The spaceship, with its silver and gold sides, its hundreds of portholes, glitters invitingly in the sun.

If you accept that it's your destiny to go with these people, turn to page 131.

If you decide not to go, turn to page 134.

Manuel appears out of nowhere. He stands before you and smiles.

"Well, my friend, found more than you bargained for, didn't you?"

"Manuel, what's going on?"

"I am an envoy from Cosmos Three. We are gathering all the brightest, most creative people from various Earth centers. They come with us to a new world. Soon, these Mayan centers will be empty. Once the leaders have gone, all others will just slow down. Their civilization will collapse."

"That's terrible!" you exclaim angrily.

Manuel looks at you and says, "People are born on earth and given a chance to prove themselves. Those that do, move on. Those that don't, well . . ."

Manuel explains your choices.

You can return to modern times and help choose people for departure to Cosmos Three.
Turn to page 124.

Or you can return to Chichen Itza and wait until a second chance comes your way—if it ever does.
Turn to page 126.

You decide to go it alone. It is a tight squeeze. Without the protection of the wet suit you would be bruised and cut as you inch through the narrow opening in the sharp rocks. At one point you think you are not going to make it.

Finally you are inside the cave. You remove the aqualung and head toward the treasure hoard.

IT'S GONE! Someone got there before you. You stand there empty handed, feeling foolish and disappointed.

Time waits for no one. . . .

The End

Finding divers and underwater salvage equipment in the Yucatan is not easy. After a long disappointing week, you find a group of professional divers in Merida. You lead them to the cave.

They place a small dynamite charge in the cave entrance. You all go back to the surface, and climb out, standing at the edge of the *cenote.* There is a muffled roar, the water foams and bubbles, and grows mucky with sand and earth. The cave mouth is free and open. The treasure is where you remembered it being. You start bringing up the gold.

Then a jeep arrives. Four uniformed Mexican officials get out.

"Congratulations! You have found the lost jewels of the Mayas. Our government will be very happy with your work." The man smiles. The other three start loading the gold and gems into their jeep.

You realize that you don't really mind, after all. The Mayan treasure rightfully belongs to the people of Mexico, who are their descendants. You are glad that you were able to restore the treasure to its real owners. And you like being the center of attention. The government invites you to Mexico City and honors you at a dinner in the Mexican Natural History Museum where the jewels will be displayed.

The End

The road to Merida is narrow, dusty and bumpy. It is so hot that even with all windows open the breeze cannot cool you. You are worried about your new job as a double agent, and the ride makes you even more nervous. Every face on the bus seems to be staring at you. You wonder if they know that you are an agent of the police. You get a creepy feeling up and down your spine.

Once you are in Merida, you place a call to a man who runs a jewelry shop. His name is Julio. As the police suggested, he is the contact for the Red Hand gang. To your surprise, they are a fine group of people. They believe that they must fight so that the poor can have land to farm and a chance to make a good living. They tell you about the government that favors the rich and punishes the poor. They welcome you into their ranks.

Late one night as you sit around a table in the cellar of an old hotel, you feel that now is the time for a decision. Should you join them, tell them who you are, and become a *triple* agent feeding the police the wrong information, or should you continue on as a spy in their midst? So far you have only heard talk, you have seen no proof of their dedication to the poor.

If you believe them and decide to fight for their cause, turn to page 108.

If you don't believe them and decide to spy on them, turn to page 109.

As you sail to the island of Cozumel, you decide that it is foolish to get involved in the politics and problems of another country. You could be killed by either side. So, once you get to Cozumel, you go right to the airport, buy a ticket, and fly back home.

As the plane lifts off from the runway you look down at this beautiful Caribbean Island, and as you speed away, it feels as if you had been to a movie. An hour later you are in Miami, Florida, and the adventure is over.

The End

You are exhausted. You didn't bargain for storms at sea, or fights with priests, or raids on neighboring towns. Your head spins at the thought of the places you have been and the things you have done. You could use a rest after all that you have been through. The Arawak Indians are a peaceful people who gather fruit from the jungle and take fish from the sea.

A month passes. You are tanned by the sun, and you used the time to organize your notes to prepare to write the book. Luckily for you the notebook was not lost at sea. But now it is time to go on. You can choose to return to Chichen Itza or go down the coast of the Yucatan and visit Tulumn. Tulumn has the romance of the sea, and Chichen Itza the mystery of the jungle.

If you return to Chichen Itza, turn to page 117.

If you go to Tulumn, turn to page 119.

Once again the order comes to cast off, and your boat heads toward the coast of Yucatan. The sea is still rough, but the worst is over now. The night sky is clear, and the stars are your points for navigation. The captain and the crew know a great deal about the stars. The Mayas have learned about the constellations and the planets, especially Venus which is both the evening and the morning star.

You put into a small fishing village for new supplies, and then continue on up the coast, stopping at settlements trading one thing for another. Weeks pass, and the life is a pleasant one. It is so pleasant, in fact, that you decide never to return to modern times. You forget about bustling cities, deadlines, inflation, and pollution. This is the life for you. Modern times are too complex.

But what happens if the time potion wears off?

If you fight the potion wearing off,
turn to page 120.

If you let things take their course,
turn to page 121.

Talk as you might, no one will join you to go to any of the towns where there is sickness. You want to convince them to bury the dead, burn down the houses and huts, cover the garbage with earth. Everyone thinks you are crazy.

"The gods are angry with us," they tell you. "There is nothing that we can do. It is said that we will all die. Maybe it is our time." You hear this over and over again.

"But we have to do something. We can't let all these people die." You plead with two priests.

"Go away. It is the will of the gods that these people will die. Leave us alone. The sickness hasn't come here yet, maybe we have pleased the gods."

Then two days later it happens. A woman takes sick and dies in one day. Then two men get the sickness. Children fall easy prey to the plague. Life in the once busy town comes to an end as the sickness sweeps through, actually wiping out the population.

Lucky for you the time potion prevents the plague from getting you. But it is time to leave. You call for Manuel to return you to the present. Your notebook is full. There is much to write about.

The End

You consider going north to alert the villagers about the plague. Fortunately a ship is setting out. The captain is willing to take you aboard.

For days your boat travels up the coast, avoiding the small towns. The captain wants no chance of landing in a place where there is plague.

Finally you reach the coast close to Chichen Itza. You arrange to be taken through the jungle to the city. Once there, you beg the priests to take sanitary measures to prevent the spread of the plague. They regard you with dislike and fear. They won't hear of your suggestions about killing rats, burning garbage, tearing down old thatch-roofed buildings, or boiling the water. They warn you to leave or they will kill you for interfering with their beliefs.

"You are evil. You must not interfere with the normal way of the world." It is the head priest.

If only Camilla were here to help or Manuel or Dr. Lopez. But they aren't. You are alone.

If you obey the priests and leave quietly, turn to page 122.

If you ignore their threats, turn to page 123.

You started out as a writer in search of the Mayas, but now you are a member of the revolutionary Red Hand gang. You and your group do not use violence to reach your goals. You don't kidnap people, you don't hijack planes, you don't blow up buildings. Instead, you talk with the people. You encourage them to demand elections, to demand land reform. You teach them about Mexican law and how to use it. You give them hope and belief. But the work is dangerous. There are people who want to stop the Red Hand at any cost.

Your life is in constant danger. But you are committed to your work as a revolutionary.

The End

You have heard of revolutionaries before, and you don't believe this group is really interested in the people. You suspect they keep the money they collect at the meetings.

When you refuse to go on a mission chosen for you, they suddenly turn on you.

"You are a spy! You are our enemy."

They tie you up. The ropes bite into your wrists. Blood dampens the hemp. After two days, when your bones ache and your body wants to cry out for help, they come to you. "You are too dangerous to let go. We have held a meeting. We are sorry, but you must die."

Go on to page 110.

In the morning you face a firing squad.

The End

You approach the group. They are frightened by your appearance. Your clothes of bright red and yellow cloth, your wristwatch, your notebook, the fact that you wear shoes, amaze them. When you speak, they look frightened and withdraw quickly. But several of the men raise their clubs and hunting spears, and approach you.

You can't communicate with them. They can't understand you, nor you them. It is like trying to teach a cat how to play checkers. Where do you begin when there isn't a language you both can use?

The End

You drain the bottle of time potion. You zoom forward, screech to a halt in the year 1208 AD and settle down in a busy Mayan market center.

Wow, have the people progressed! They are chattering away, bargaining over food and cloth. They have developed a mathematical system, they have built huge and artistically designed temples, they understand the stars in the sky. They have a calendar.

People no longer wander in search of food, but instead live in permanent settlements. Children are trained in crafts and in the skills of simple math and writing. Pottery and jewelry are valued.

For you, it is time to go. A glimpse of the past is interesting, but the closest you get to the mystery of what happened to the Mayas later on is the idea that droughts, overpopulation, and warfare wiped them out.

What more can you do? There is nothing more you can learn from your journeys into the past. You decide that you must write up your notes, reread the books written by others about the Mayas, and then you can write your own interpretation of what happened.

The End

You enter the Region of Light. It is like being inside a giant dome made of soda straws connected by red, yellow, blue, silver and green balls. Lights flow through the giant straws. The balls gleam and shine. You hear strange music that sounds like the rushing of air through the pines, the smacking of ocean on the beaches, the cries of animals in happiness and pain. You have been chosen to understand the universe.

You are sent back to earth to be a guide for those who search and wonder. It is not presented as a choice. It is a command.

The End

115

The Planet of Dreams is like a giant amusement park. There are fun houses, haunted caves, space rides, movie theaters. Nothing is real. You don't like the Planet of Dreams. It disturbs you. You would rather return to the real world, as hard as it may be.

As you stand in front of a movie theatre, a man wearing the uniform of a peanut vendor comes up to you. It is Dr. Lopez! He speaks. "Well, we get what we want. If you want to be a dreamer, you get it. If not, you can change. Time to go now."

You decide to go to the Region of Light.

Turn to page 114.

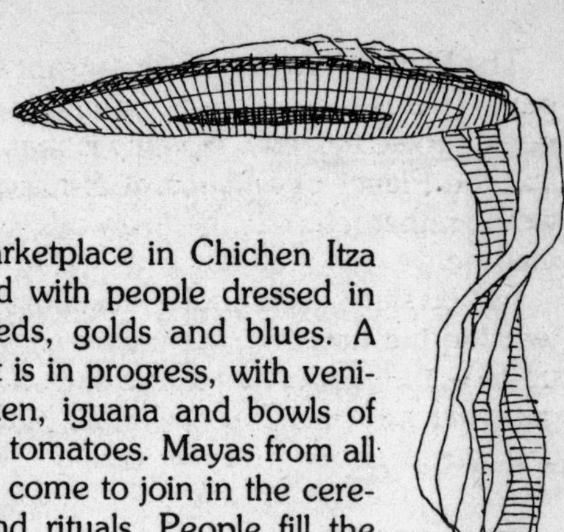

The marketplace in Chichen Itza is crowded with people dressed in brilliant reds, golds and blues. A great feast is in progress, with venison, chicken, iguana and bowls of maize and tomatoes. Mayas from all over have come to join in the ceremonies and rituals. People fill the enormous courtyards, chanting and singing.

Priests march about, followed by attendants. Warriors gather in groups, standing rigidly, looking fierce and stern.

Go on to page 118.

At the sound of a huge gong, the crowds fall silent. The priests march through the throngs to El Castillo—the great pyramid. They mount the steps. At the top of the steps the head priest raises his arms to the sun, and at that precise moment the moon passes in front of the sun. Sudden darkness envelops the area. People are frightened. The priest drops his arms. When the sun once again shines as the moon continues its course, the people cheer. The ceremony has been a success.

You watch, amused by the way the priests have used knowledge of a solar eclipse to impress their people. Knowledge can be power.

Time now for you to go. You have looked at the Mayas, seen many things, but the question of why they disappeared still remains a mystery. You will write about each theory with authority, but you will conclude that there is no one reason for the collapse of the Mayan civilization.

Several years later your book is published. You receive good reviews. You spend your time now traveling around the country, giving lectures on the Mayan Indians.

The End

You set off with a guide for Tulumn. Late one evening, you are sitting next to your fire near a small rocky hill. Thick brush surrounds you. Without warning a band of warriors rushes at you. Arrows fill the air. Your guide is killed. You fight back as best you can, knocking down two of your attackers with stones. Then you run. But an arrow hits you in the side. It's a poisoned arrow. Everything grows hazy, blurry, distant. The world seems to be spinning about your head. Your tongue feels thick and dry. There is darkness. You are finished.

The End

There must be some way to stay in the past! You just can't go back to the modern world!

The time potion wears off little by little. One day you look around and all your new friends begin to fade slightly. They become less distinct each day, until finally there is no one around you. You are alone. You are sitting on the sand listening to the waves crash on the beach.

"Help, Help! I don't want to be here."

There is no one to hear you.

The End

What did you expect? You really can't hold onto the past. Time moves. You were given a glimpse into the past—but only a glimpse. You belong to the present and the future.

For you, your journey to the past has ended. The present and the future are before you.

The End

The priests are too powerful to fool around with. They are in charge, and even the chief bows to their will. It has not always been that way; the priests were respected, but the chief and his advisers were the actual rulers until recent time. Now, when the people are frightened by something like the plague, the priests and their predictions about the future become very important.

The people are frightened now. They move away from Chichen Itza in groups with a few belongings. Some head south to the jungles and the low-lying hills. Others go to the coast, and still others go west.

The feast days and ceremonies at the great pyramids and the games in the ball court draw fewer and fewer people now. Fear has done its work better than the actual plague. The lifeblood of Chichen Itza drains away as the people leave searching for a better future.

The End

You won't leave. Immediately you go to the chief who rules the area. He lives in a huge palace, surrounded by servants. Six guards try to stop you; after all, you look like one of the field laborers. But the chief overhears your argument with the guards as he leaves the main room to go outside.

"Let this person come in," he says.

Then you are standing in front of this powerful man.

"Well, what do you have to say?"

"I want to help. I know how we can stop this sickness."

You explain that the sickness can be stopped if rats are killed, water boiled, and the garbage is buried. He listens intently and agrees to give it careful thought. These are new ideas, and he isn't sure that they will work.

But it is too late. The plague has spread, and soon Chichen Itza is filled with sickness.

You have witnessed one of the reasons for the decline of the Mayas. You are safe because you are only a time traveler and soon you return to the present. Dr. Lopez greets you in Merida saying, "The Mayas were great people, but all civilizations fall one day."

The End

Cosmos Three? What a bizarre idea. You look into the sky. You realize that the sun is but one small star among billions in the universe. Why not? Why not prepare to live elsewhere? Maybe Earth is a school planet—a nursery for other realms.

You turn to Manuel and say: "I'll do it. But how?"

He takes a small object from his pocket. It looks like a pocket calculator; but the buttons on it are different from anything that you have ever seen. They have signs on them that are half numbers and half letters.

"Everything you need to know is stored in here. Just follow a preprogrammed ritual. Hold the communicator in your left hand, chest high, face Venus—morning and evening star—and the information and instructions will flow into you. Good-bye, good luck."

You find yourself standing on the street in Chicago. You are almost run over by a car. The driver yells at you:

"Hey, stupid, are you tryin' ta get killed?"

You smile because you know that your real work is just beginning. You will find the best people and prepare them for departure to the new world.

The End

Chichen Itza is just as you left it. Laborers come and go in the hot fields, harvesting grain and melons and squash. People in the shops and buildings near the temple barter for goods, work on carvings, eat in the small shops where food is sold. Excitement and energy fill the air. You enjoy watching this way of life. You are a careful observer, and your notebook fills with accurate details of Mayan life. Occasionally you wish that you had gone on the spaceship, but those thoughts pass. You are satisfied to live in the past for a short time, knowing that one day you will return to the present and tell the world what you have learned.

The End

Red leads to a job with the workers at the Pyramid of the Moon. You are shown how to chip and carve the delicate patterns in stone that decorate the hallways and secret chambers of this magnificent pyramid. Heads of serpents, fierce faces with bulging eyes, and feathered birds, are carved in stone.

All day you hammer and chip, following lines drawn on the stone by the Toltec priest-artists. Fine stone dust clogs your mouth and nose. Your eyes water constantly.

Then one day you are amazed to see six people in modern drip-dry clothes walking toward you. One of them waves. Then they all wave. You run toward them but are stopped by an invisible wall of time.

You can't get back to the present time. Forever more, you must chip away at the stone carvings in the great Pyramid of the Moon.

The End

Blue is a magic color. Only one of the straws was colored blue! You are now chosen to be a messenger to the Toltec god, Smoking Mirror.

Dressed in royal robes of blue and red, you are led to the top of the Pyramid of the Sun, tied to a small stone table, and left to meet Smoking Mirror.

It's the end for you. You are to be sacrificed.

The End

You are the mighty ruler, inheritor of the Plumed Serpent. Beware any and all who defy you. You enter Chichen Itza triumphantly. Wherever you go, people recognize you as their new ruler. You are worshipped and loved.

Great feasts are held in the courtyard and thousands of people join in. When the ball game is played, however, you refuse to let the loser be sacrificed. You stop all sacrifices of people and animals, replacing them with offerings of maize and squash and chili peppers. The people love you and respect you, but the priests grow sullen and angry. They dislike you because you have taken away their power. Too bad for them, you think. The people count. Not a bad accomplishment for a struggling writer.

The End

The snakebite hurts. The Plumed Serpent becomes a simple dangerous snake again. It slides over the tree trunk, tucks its head in a hole, and vanishes.

It's all over. The Toltecs leave you on the spot to die. You are useless to them now.

But you don't die! The Plumed Serpent was protecting you all along. The spirit of the Plumed Serpent makes you well again. And you live on as one of the attendants of the most powerful of the Mayan gods.

The End

Cruzora was right. You stay with these friendly people. It is all like a dream to you, you feel that whatever you do is correct. Nothing can hurt you. You no longer feel lonely or lost or worried. You are at peace.

By nightfall, all have gathered aboard the spacecraft. With no noise and with no feeling of movement, you and your new companions leave earth. The acceleration is fantastic. Earth becomes a tiny pinpoint dot in just three seconds. The planets Mars and Jupiter flash by in less than a minute. You break out of the Milky Way galaxy and head for intergalactic space.

The End

You drew yellow. It is the straw of the ruler. You are immediately made the new ruler of the Toltecs. You rule until you die of old age at 93. Several times Manuel and Dr. Lopez try to get you to go back to the present, but you refuse. You enjoy being the ruler.

The End

Hesitation prevents you from joining this band of adventurers and explorers. You stand by and watch them as they cheerfully climb aboard the spacecraft. Is it a dream? One moment it is there; the next it is gone. You are totally alone, and the only evidence that remains is a mark on the earth where the group of people had been before getting on board. You stare in wonder into the sky. It is morning, and you see Venus high above you. Maybe next time you will go.

The End

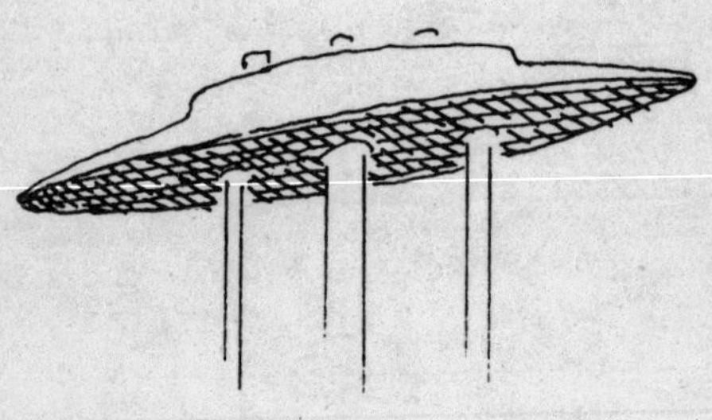

ABOUT THE AUTHOR

R. A. Montgomery is an educator and publisher. A graduate of Williams College, he also studied in graduate programs at Yale University and New York University. After serving in a variety of administrative capacities at Williston Academy and Columbia University, he co-founded the Waitsfield Summer School in 1965. Following that, Montgomery helped found a research and development firm specializing in the development of educational programs. He worked for several years as a consultant to the Peace Corps in Washington, D.C. and West Africa. For the last five years, he has been both a writer and a publisher.